MW00744376

Dwight D. Eisenhower

BY MIRELLA S. MILLER

Published by The Child's World®
1980 Lookout Drive • Mankato, MN 56003-1705
800-599-READ • www.childsworld.com

ISBN 9781503816442
LCCN 2016945624

Printed in the United States of America
PAO2322

ABOUT THE AUTHOR

Mirella S. Miller is an author and
editor of several children's books. She
lives in Minnesota with her husband
and their dog.

Table of Contents

Eisenhower was a famous U.S. Army general of World War II.

CHAPTER ONE

D-Day Decisions

It was the night of June 5, 1944. World War II was being fought around the world. General Dwight D. Eisenhower was nervous. A **military** attack was planned for June 6. U.S. and **Allied** troops would fight in France. They wanted to stop the **Nazis**. The Nazis were spreading through Europe. Adolf Hitler was their leader. He killed millions of people. Hitler wanted to take over the world.

Eisenhower spent more than a year preparing. Other military **officials** helped him.

The attack would cost a lot of money. More than one million Allied soldiers would fight. They needed many weapons. This would be one of the biggest attacks in history.

Eisenhower had to make a decision. He had to decide if troops would fight. The weather was stormy and cloudy. This made it harder to attack. Troops would hit from the air and water. Eisenhower knew soldiers would die. But the Nazis needed to be stopped. He decided the troops would continue as planned.

Eisenhower's decision paid off. The Nazis gave up less than one year later. World War II ended. June 6 became known as D-Day. Many people called Eisenhower a hero. Americans loved him. His **popularity** led to other important jobs. Eisenhower would become president of the United States.

Eisenhower gave orders to soldiers before the attack on Normandy, France, on June 6, 1944.

Ike as a child with three of his brothers, from left to right, Roy, Arthur, Edgar, and Ike

CHAPTER TWO

Eisenhower's Early Life

★ ★ ★

Dwight David Eisenhower was born on October 14, 1890. He was from Denison, Texas. He was the third of seven boys. His family called him "Ike." The family moved to Kansas in 1891. Ike's father fixed machines for a living. He made sure they ran properly. His family did not have a lot of money. The sons had to work hard. They did many chores.

Ike enjoyed sports more than schoolwork. He played football and baseball. Ike also hunted and fished. He liked reading about military history.

Ike graduated high school in 1909. He began working seven days a week. Ike worked for two years. He paid for his brother Edgar to go to college. After two years, Edgar was supposed to work. Then he would pay for college for Ike. Ike went to West Point instead. This is a military school in New York. Ike's mother did not believe in war. She was sad to see Ike go.

Ike played football at West Point. But he hurt his knee his second year. He had to stop playing. Ike still liked having fun more than studying. He finished in the middle of his class. He graduated in 1915. Then the military sent Ike to Texas. There he trained soldiers. This was the start of his successful career.

Ike played as a running back on the
West Point football team.

Eisenhower and Mamie were married at her parent's home in Denver, Colorado.

CHAPTER THREE

Military Experience

Eisenhower worked a few jobs after graduation. One was training tank crews. A war was happening during this time. It was World War I. Eisenhower was going to go to Europe to fight. But the war ended before he left.

Big changes were happening in Eisenhower's life during this time. He met Mamie Doud. They married in 1916. Their first son was born in 1917. His name was Doud. Doud became sick. He died in 1921.

Mamie gave birth to another son in 1922. His name was John.

Soon Eisenhower started a new job. He worked at the Panama Canal Zone. He did this until 1924. Then he was picked to attend a special school. It was an advanced military school in Kansas. He graduated first in his class in 1926.

Eisenhower served in France in the late 1920s. Then he served in Washington, DC. In 1933, he traveled to the Philippines. He worked with General Douglas MacArthur. MacArthur was an important U.S. Army leader. The United States helped the Philippines build an army. Eisenhower won an award for his work.

Eisenhower went back to Washington, DC. It was 1941. The United States had entered World War II. Eisenhower was a planning officer.

Eisenhower worked alongside MacArthur
(left) in the Philippines for three years.

He worked hard. Many people noticed. This led to important jobs. He moved up quickly in the military.

Eisenhower was leading troops in Europe by 1944. D-Day helped the Allies win World War II. The war ended in 1945. People saw Eisenhower as a strong leader. Americans called him a hero.

Then Eisenhower became president of Columbia University. That is in New York. He worked there for two years. Then the Korean War started. President Harry S. Truman asked Eisenhower to help. Eisenhower left the university. He commanded troops during the war.

Eisenhower came home after the war. Many Americans wondered what was next for him. He said he would run for president. The **Republican** Party chose him as their **candidate**.

Eisenhower (left) ate with soldiers while
in Korea on December 1, 1952.

Eisenhower and Mamie celebrated his presidential victory on November 5, 1952.

CHAPTER FOUR

Becoming President

★ ★ ★

It was November 4, 1952. Eisenhower won the **election**. He became the 34th president of the United States. Eisenhower got to work right away. He created a peace agreement by July 1953. It ended the Korean War. He also passed an important law. It helped more Americans save money for retirement.

Eisenhower finished his first **term** in 1956. He was popular. Americans elected him again. He created new programs for the country. One was a big highway project.

More than 41,000 miles (66,000 km) of roads were built. This road was called the Interstate Highway. It made traveling long distances faster.

In 1957, Eisenhower signed a civil rights law. Civil rights are rights all humans should have. They are not based on race or gender. This law protected African Americans' voting rights.

Americans remember Eisenhower's presidency as happy years. The **economy** was growing. People had money. They bought cars and TVs. They spent more money on clothes and activities.

Eisenhower left the White House in 1961. He moved back to his farm. It was in Gettysburg, Pennsylvania. He helped later presidents when they had questions. He traveled and painted. He also wrote a few books. Eisenhower was sick for many years. He died on March 28, 1969.

Then-president Richard Nixon (right) sat with Eisenhower on February 2, 1969, a month before he died.

People around the world looked up to Eisenhower. He was an American hero. He helped end a war. He wanted peace in the world. Many Americans were sad when he passed away. Eisenhower's work helped many people.

1890

←— **October 14, 1890** Dwight D. Eisenhower is born in Denison, Texas.

←— **June 12, 1915** Eisenhower graduates from West Point.

←— **July 1, 1916** Eisenhower marries Mamie Geneva Doud.

←— **September 24, 1917** Doud Dwight Eisenhower is born. He dies from scarlet fever in 1921.

←— **January 1922** Eisenhower begins work in the Panama Canal Zone.

←— **August 3, 1922** John Sheldon Doud Eisenhower is born.

←— **September 1935** Eisenhower begins working with General Douglas MacArthur.

←— **June 6, 1944** Eisenhower commands the Allied invasion in Normandy, France, during World War II.

←— **December 16, 1950** Eisenhower is named the commander in Europe during the Korean War.

←— **November 4, 1952** Eisenhower is elected 34th president of the United States.

←— **November 6, 1956** Voters reelect Eisenhower as president for a second term.

←— **January 20, 1961** Eisenhower's second term as president ends.

←— **March 28, 1969** Eisenhower dies at age 78.

1970

Allied (AL-ide) Allied troops were the countries, including the United States, that fought against the Axis powers in World War II. Eisenhower led the Allied troops in Europe.

candidate (KAN-duh-date) A candidate is a person trying to be elected to office. Eisenhower was the Republican presidential candidate in 1952.

economy (i-KON-uh-mee) The economy is a system through which goods and services are sold and bought. The economy was growing while Eisenhower was president.

election (i-LEK-shuhn) An election is when people choose a leader by voting. Eisenhower won his first presidential election in 1952.

military (MIL-uh-ter-ee) The military is a group made up of armed forces. Eisenhower led a military attack in France on June 6, 1945.

Nazis (NOT-sees) Nazis were members of Germany's major political party from the 1920s to the 1940s. Adolf Hitler led the Nazis.

officials (uh-FISH-uhls) Officials are people who hold authority. Military officials helped Eisenhower create an attack plan.

popularity (pop-yuh-LAYR-it-ee) Popularity is a state of being liked by many people. Eisenhower gained popularity while he was president.

Republican (ri-PUHB-li-kuhn) A Republican is a member of the Republican political party in the United States. Eisenhower was a Republican.

term (TERM) A term is a period of time an official serves in office. Eisenhower was elected for a second presidential term in 1956.

In the Library

Aronin, Miriam. *Dwight D. Eisenhower.* New York: Bearport, 2016.

Cawthorne, Nigel. *Victory: 100 Great Military Commanders.* New York: Metro, 2012.

Hansen, Sarah. *Dwight D. Eisenhower.* Mankato, MN: The Child's World, 2009.

On the Web

Visit our Web site for links about
Dwight D. Eisenhower: **childsworld.com/links**

Note to Parents, Teachers, and Librarians: We routinely verify our Web links to make sure they are safe and active sites. So encourage your readers to check them out!

INDEX